I Love You Bigger Than The Sky!

Written by Sharon Denise Talbot

Illustrated by Laura Ashley Talbot

Love Big,
Sharon Denise Talbot
2015

First Edition: March 2010

ISBN 978-1450591119

Published by

RubyRedRiter Enterprises

P.O. Box 1783

Iowa, LA 70647

www.rubyredriter.com

For

Skylar Dru & Sydney Cate

"I love you bigger than the sky!"

Mammy

I love you **bigger** than the sky,

bigger than the moon,

Even **bigger** than the very **biggest** red balloon!

I love you **more** than candy apples,

more than chocolate cake,

Even **more** than the sugar cookies that we like to make!

I love you **higher** than the buildings,

higher than the water shooting up from the fountain,

Even **higher** than the **highest** of all the mountains!

I love you **better** than really fun toys,

better than a basketful of yummy, yummy treats,

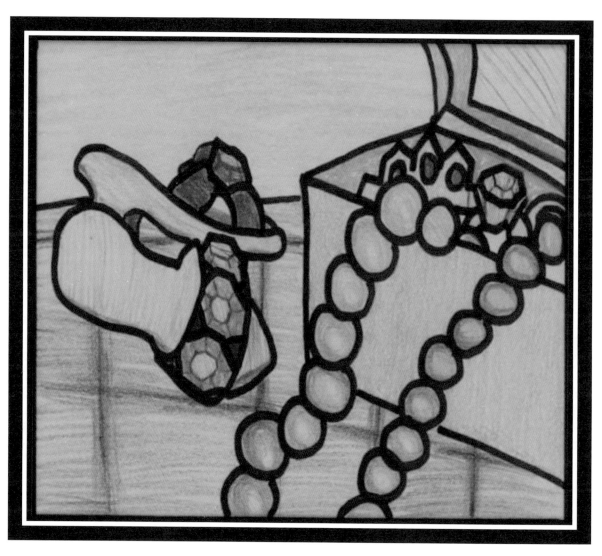

Even **better** than lots of sparkly jewelry and pretty shoes for my feet!

I love you **greater** than a hippo or rhino,

greater than a whale,

Even **greater** than a dinosaur with a great big tail!

I love you **larger** than an elephant,

larger than a house,

Even **larger**, really **large**, not small like a mouse!

I love you, I love you!

Dr. Pepper and pizza pie.

I love you! I love you **bigger** than the sky!

Acknowledgements

Dr. Pepper is canned by a member of the Coca-Cola Bottlers' Association,

Atlanta GA 30327

Under the authority of Dr. Pepper Company, Plano, TX 75024

© 2008 Dr. Pepper/Seven Up, Inc.

Special thanks to:

My husband, Mark

and

my children, Sarah, Laura & Matt

for always believing in me

and

Dwayne Coots

for giving me the opportunity to believe in myself.

Made in the USA
San Bernardino, CA
24 September 2014